# THE BOY WHO WAS BROUGHT UP BY TEDDY BEARS

Text copyright © 2001 by Jeanne Willis. Illustration copyright © 2001 by Susan Varley.
This special paperback edition first published in 2003 by Andersen Press Ltd.
The rights of Jeanne Willis and Susan Varley to be identified as the author and illustrator of this work
have been asserted by them in accordance with the Copyright, Designs and Patents Act, 1988.
First published in Great Britain in 2001 by Andersen Press Ltd. 20 Vauxhall Bridge Road, London SW1V 2SA.
Published in Australia by Random House Australia Pty., 20 Alfred Street, Milsons Point, Sydney, NSW 2061.
All rights reserved. Colour separated in Switzerland by Photolitho AG, Zürich.
Printed and bound in China.

10  9  8  7  6  5  4  3  2  1

British Library Cataloguing in Publication Data available.

ISBN 1 84270 255 6

This book has been printed on acid-free paper

# THE BOY WHO WAS BROUGHT UP BY TEDDY BEARS

A fairy tale by **Jeanne Willis**

with pictures by **Susan Varley**

Ⓐ

Andersen Press · London

Once there was a little boy
who was brought up by Teddy Bears.
They found him in the woods, in his pram,
when he was a baby.

"Where's his mother?" wondered Big Teddy.
"Where's his father?" wondered Middle Teddy.
"I can't see them anywhere!" said Little Teddy.
So, thinking the baby was all alone in the world,
they carried him back to their cottage.

When they got home, the baby began to cry.
"He's hungry. Let's give him some sawdust," said Big Teddy.
"He's thirsty. Let's give him some pond water," said Middle Teddy.
"He's lonely. Let's give him a name," said Little Teddy.

They didn't know any People Names,
so they gave him Teddy names instead.
"I shall call him Pinky, because he's pink," said Big Teddy.
"I shall call him Blinky, because he blinks," said Middle Teddy.
"And I shall call him Dinky," said Little Teddy,
"because he's so little."

The Teddy Bears weren't sure whether to keep him or not.

"I think I should take him to the police," said Big Teddy.
"I think I should take him to hospital," said Middle Teddy.
"I think I should take him to bed," said Little Teddy.
Little Teddy got into bed and cuddled the baby
and it smiled and went fast to sleep.

The days turned into weeks . . .

. . . the weeks turned into years,
and all this time Pinky Blinky Dinky
was looked after by Teddy Bears.

He walked like a Teddy. He growled like a Teddy.
He could even swivel his legs all the way around . . . almost.

Grrrr

He slept in cupboards . . .

He sat on shelves . . .

He went to more picnics than you've had hot dinners.

He even dressed like a Teddy
and tied a red ribbon round his neck
with an enormous bow at the front.

And, of course, he was very cuddly.

For three whole years,
Pinky Blinky Dinky truly believed
he was a Teddy Bear.
"We have to tell him the truth,"
said Big Teddy.
"It might upset him,"
said Middle Teddy.
"He'll find out soon enough,"
said Little Teddy.

And so he did. On Pinky's fourth birthday,
there was a knock at the door.
It was his real mother.

"I'm searching for my long lost son," she said.
"He vanished from his pram when he was a baby.
Do you think the fairies might have taken him?"

"It wasn't the fairies," said Big Teddy.
"It was someone else," said Middle Teddy.
"It was us . . ." said Little Teddy.

And sure enough, there was Pinky Blinky Dinky,
lying with his legs in the air, upside down on the Teddy Bears' sofa!

"Edward!"
cried his mother. "My boy!"
"What's a boy?" said Pinky.
His mother tried to explain.

"But I don't want to be a boy!" he said.
"I want to be a Teddy Bear. I want to hide in cupboards
and go on picnics and play in the woods with my friends."
"Boys are allowed to do those things too," said his mother.
"But are boys allowed to have . . . cuddles?" he asked.
"Oh yes!" said his mother and she gave him
the biggest bear hug he'd ever had.

"I wish I could have a hug like that,"
sighed Big Teddy.
"So do I," said Middle Teddy.
"Me too!" said Little Teddy.

"Come here then," said Mum.
And she cuddled them all the way home.